CW00842981

First published as *Olly and Me* (2004)
by Walker Books Ltd, 87 Vauxhall Walk, London SE11 5HJ

Additional artwork from *Out and About* (1988), *The Nursery Collection* (1994),
Let's Join In (1998) and *Olly and Me, 123* (2009)

This edition published 2020

2 4 6 8 10 9 7 5 3 1

© 1988–2020 Shirley Hughes

Introduction © 2020 Shirley Hughes
Additional text by Walker Books Ltd

The right of Shirley Hughes to be identified as author/illustrator
of this work has been asserted by her in accordance with
the Copyright, Designs and Patents Act 1988

This book has been typeset in Sabon and Plantin

Printed in China

All rights reserved. No part of this book may be reproduced, transmitted
or stored in an information retrieval system in any form or by any means, graphic,
electronic or mechanical, including photocopying, taping and recording,
without prior written permission from the publisher.

British Library Cataloguing in Publication Data:
a catalogue record for this book is available
from the British Library

ISBN: 978-1-4063-9527-3

www.walker.co.uk

All recipes are for informational and/or entertainment purposes only;
please check ingredients carefully if you have any allergies and, if in doubt, consult
a health professional. Adult supervision required for all recipes.

TIME FOR TEA
A FIRST BOOK OF COOKERY

Shirley Hughes

WALKER BOOKS
AND SUBSIDIARIES
LONDON · BOSTON · SYDNEY · AUCKLAND

CONTENTS

A NOTE FROM SHIRLEY HUGHES

This book is a gentle introduction to food and cookery for children, inspired by Olly and Katie's everyday adventures through the year. Cooking can be so much fun and there is so much to taste, smell and see when you're being creative with food. Some of these recipes have quite a few steps, so please do make sure there is always an adult on hand to help you make your teatime treats. I hope my readers will enjoy making these recipes and reading all about Olly and Katie along the way.

Shirley Hughes

THINGS YOU NEED TO DO:

- Always ask an adult to help you with each step of every recipe.
- Read the recipes carefully, especially if you have any allergies.
- Wash fruit, vegetables and salad.
- Wash and dry your hands before touching food.
- Wear an apron to protect your clothes.
- Be creative and have lots of fun!

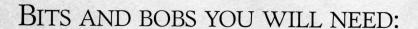

BITS AND BOBS YOU WILL NEED:

- Baking paper
- Baking tray
- Child-friendly knife
- Chopping board
- Cupcake cases
- 12-hole cupcake tray
- Kitchen scales
- Large mixing bowl
- Measuring jug
- Pastry brush
- Rolling pin
- Teaspoon and tablespoon
- Whisk
- Wire cooling rack
- Wooden spoon

Pancake Day

When Mum goes out and Dad looks after Olly and Katie, they often do cooking. Making pancakes with Dad is quite exciting. He cracks open the eggs and Olly and Katie help him stir up the sticky stuff. Then Dad does the frying.

The most exciting part is when he picks up the pan and flips the pancake into the air and catches it. It is even more exciting when he misses and some of the pancake goes on the floor.

Their dog Buster likes that. But eating pancakes rolled up with plenty of honey is the part they like best of all.

Honey pancakes

Making pancakes is so much fun. Once the batter is in the pan, ask an adult to flip the pancake in the air!

Ingredients:
100 g plain flour
250 ml milk
50 ml water
A large egg
A little butter
A squeeze of honey
Makes 6

You will need:
A mixing bowl
A non-stick frying pan
A whisk
A tablespoon

Method

1. Tip the flour into a bowl, pour in the milk and water, then carefully crack in the egg and whisk the mixture into a smooth batter.

2. Ask an adult to add a little butter to a frying pan and heat, then carefully spoon in some of the pancake mixture and swirl it around the pan so that it makes a thin circular shape.

3. When the pancake is golden on one side, ask an adult to flip it and cook the other side, then tip it onto a plate for you.

4. When the pancake has cooled a little, add a squeeze of honey and carefully roll it up. Keep making pancakes until all of the mix is used.

Super smoothies

*Mash soft fruits with some milk and yogurt
to make these super tasty smoothies.*

Ingredients:
A banana
6 strawberries
2 teaspoons of honey
A tablespoon of natural yogurt
A glass of milk
Makes 2

You will need:
A chopping board
A knife
A large mixing bowl
A potato masher
2 cups for serving

Method

1. Peel half of the banana and wash the strawberries, making sure to remove any stalks. With an adult to help you, chop the strawberries and half the banana on a chopping board, then put in a mixing bowl.

2. Using a masher, mash the fruit until it turns into a pulp.

3. Add the honey and yogurt into the bowl and stir. Then add the milk and mix all of the ingredients together.

4. Ask an adult to help you pour or spoon the mixture into two cups and chop the other half of the banana into thick slices. Gently push a couple of banana slices over the rim of each cup to decorate and enjoy!

Stories Galore

Olly and Katie have lots
of books. Olly likes chewing
his, but he stops doing it when
Katie shows him the pictures.
Down at the library there are stories galore.
Olly and Katie go there on Saturday afternoons.

While Mum is choosing her book, Dad and Olly and Katie sit on cushions on the floor while a lady tells them all about the Three Little Pigs and the Owl and the Pussycat and the Billy Goats Gruff. And Olly sits still and listens without wriggling (well, most of the time, anyway).

When it's time for Katie to choose her books to take home, Dad says: "Why do you always choose the same ones?" And Katie says it's because she likes them best, of course. But one day, Katie will read all the books in the library!

Sprinkled toast

Add a touch of magic to toast by sprinkling it with some sugar and cinnamon to make a sweet and crunchy treat.

Ingredients:
A slice of bread
A little butter
A pinch of cinnamon
A pinch of sugar
Makes 1

You will need:
A knife
A plate

Method

1. Ask an adult to help toast the bread and spread a little butter onto it.

2. Sprinkle a pinch of cinnamon and sugar over the toast.

3. Ask an adult to help you cut the toast into four triangles. Enjoy!

Melon sailboats

Melons are wonderfully refreshing and melon slices make perfect sailboats.

Ingredients:
A cantaloupe melon
An orange
Makes 6

You will need:
A chopping board
A tablespoon
6 wooden lollipop sticks

Method

1. Ask an adult to cut the melon in half on a chopping board. Using your tablespoon, carefully scoop out the seeds from the middle of each half of the melon.

2. Ask an adult to cut each half of the melon into three pieces then slice the orange into six circular slices, about a centimetre thick.

3. Carefully slide a slice of orange onto the lollipop stick so that it bows out like a sail.

4. Arrange the melon pieces so that they are skin down. Push a lollipop stick into each melon piece to add the sails to your sailboats.

My Friend Betty

There's a place in the park
where the farm animals live: the pig with a house
of his own, and the hens and geese. But whenever
Olly and Katie go there, Katie always visits Betty
the sheep first.

She has a nice fat back. And when she sees Katie she
always turns her head and lets her touch her nose.

Olly likes rabbits.

When they come out of their hutch Olly and Katie are allowed to stroke them – the beautiful black one, the brown ones with silky ears and the white one with pink eyes.

But Betty is Katie's special friend.

Bobtail bites

These bite-sized treats are perfect for sharing.
They look just like the tail on Olly's rabbit!

Ingredients:
150 g white chocolate
100 g crispy rice cereal
25 g desiccated coconut
Makes 12

You will need:
A large heatproof bowl
A wooden spoon
A 12-hole cupcake tray lined
  with cupcake cases
A teaspoon

Method

1. Ask an adult to melt the chocolate in a large heatproof bowl. When the chocolate has cooled a little, carefully pour in the cereal and use a wooden spoon to mix.

2. When the cereal is all coated, sprinkle in the desiccated coconut and stir until combined.

3. Use a teaspoon to spoon the mix into the cupcake cases.

4. Pop the tray in the fridge so the bobtail bites can set.

Apple animals

Make as many kinds of animal faces as you like,
using these sweet and crunchy ingredients.

Ingredients:
A crunchy apple
A handful of raisins
A handful of crispy rice cereal
A little peanut butter or jam
Makes 4

You will need:
A chopping board
A knife
A teaspoon
A plate or small tray

Method

1. Ask an adult to slice the apple into four circular slices, about a centimetre thick.

2. Lay the slices on a plate or small tray. Use a teaspoon to spread a little peanut butter across each apple slice as glue. Then stick on the crispy rice to add eyes, nose and whiskers.

3. Ask an adult to cut ear shapes out of any leftover apple and stick in place with some more peanut butter or jam.

Car Ride

Olly and Katie are in the car
Strapped in their seats.
They sit and they sit,
Looking at other cars,
And the backs of trucks.
Olly is cross,
Bemily's feeling sick,
As they watch the lampposts
Gliding past – fast!
Like people in a long, long line.
And still they sit.
Olly sucks his thumb
And dozes off.
Katie's got her book
But she still looks
At the huge signs
(which she can't read)
And the places for petrol,
And the lampposts,
Rushing past.
And she wishes and she wishes they were there.

Then, at last,
They stop!
Olly wakes up
(Still cross)
But they're there!
They're there, in the bright air!
And they're walking on grass.

Picnic pockets

Fill these pitta pockets with as many tasty fillings as you can think of, then take some to share on a picnic!

Ingredients:
A couple of pitta breads
Your favourite sandwich fillings,
  e.g. cheese or ham
Salad leaves
A tomato (sliced)
Makes 4

You will need:
A chopping board
A knife

Method

1. Ask an adult to pop the pittas in a toaster, then leave to cool on a chopping board.

2. When they're cool enough to handle, ask an adult to slice the pitta in two and open up the pockets.

3. Put your favourite sandwich fillings into the pitta pockets, including some salad leaves and slices of fresh tomato.

Rainbow fruits

Add your favourite fruits to make this fruit salad as colourful as possible.

Ingredients:
A selection of fruit
A little orange juice
A small bunch of fresh mint
Makes 2

You will need:
A large mixing bowl
A tablespoon
A knife
2 small bowls for serving

Method

1. Ask an adult to help you carefully wash, peel and chop the fruits into bite-size pieces and add them to the bowl.

2. Pour some orange juice over the chopped fruit and stir the salad together with a tablespoon.

3. Carefully scoop a little fruit salad into each bowl. Tear some fresh mint with your hands and sprinkle it on top.

People in the Pond

Peering over the stone rim,
Olly and Katie see four faces
looking back at them:
Buster, Mum, Olly and Katie,
wobbly and green in the water.
Down below, the fish glide,
grey and silver,
pink and gold;
hovering, rising,
then suddenly diving,
with a brisk whisk of their tails,
while the little fish slip in and out like ripples.
Now their faces break up into bits of watery light.
But the boy in the middle of the pond
stands still as stone, endlessly pouring
water from his stone jar.

Pond puddings

Once you've made your pond puddings, give them
a little shake to see the jelly wobbling about.

Ingredients:
A packet of lime jelly
6 green grapes (halved)
Ice cream to serve
Makes 6

You will need:
A measuring jug
A knife
6 clear, small dishes for serving

Method

1. Ask an adult to help you make the jelly mix in a measuring jug according to the packet instructions, then carefully pour it into six small dishes.

2. Wash and dry the grapes, cut them in half, then drop two halves into each dish. Put the dishes in the fridge until the jelly sets.

3. When the pond puddings have set, ask an adult to take them out of the fridge. Serve with a little ice cream.

Nest cakes

*Add a few chocolate eggs to each of your nests
to finish off these wonderfully crunchy treats.*

Ingredients:
150 g milk chocolate
100 g cornflakes cereal
36 small chocolate eggs
Makes 12

You will need:
A heatproof bowl
A wooden spoon
A teaspoon
A 12-hole cupcake tray
  lined with cupcake cases

Method

1. Ask an adult to melt the chocolate in a heatproof bowl and leave it to cool. Once the chocolate is cool, tip in the cornflakes.

2. Stir the mix together until the cornflakes are well coated. Using your teaspoon, carefully scoop a little of the mix and pop it into a cupcake case. Repeat until all the cupcake cases are full.

3. Using the bottom of your teaspoon, make a little dent in the middle of each nest. Add three chocolate eggs to each nest, then put the nests in the fridge until they have set.

Happy Birthday, Dear Mum

Katie is colouring in a beautiful card for Mum.
Because tomorrow, when she wakes up, it will be
her birthday! Katie has tried to explain to Olly
about birthdays but he doesn't quite understand.
He can't remember his own,
but he's hoping for balloons.
They are his favourite
thing at the moment.

Katie has a present for Mum which Dad and Katie bought together. It's a keyring with a sheep on it, so she won't have to search for her keys so often.

They've got a surprise cake with candles. (But not one for every year because Dad says that grown-ups don't always have that.)

Tomorrow Mum will have breakfast in bed.
There will be lots of crushy hugs.
And presents.

Butterfly cupcakes

*These light and pretty butterfly cupcakes are perfect
for any special occasion.*

Ingredients:
150 g caster sugar
150 g butter
2 large eggs
150 g plain flour
A teaspoon of baking powder
Strawberry jam
A little icing sugar
Makes 12

You will need:
A 12-hole cupcake tray lined
  with cupcake cases
A large mixing bowl
A wooden spoon
A sieve
A wire cooling rack
A teaspoon

Method

1. Ask an adult to preheat the oven to 180°C and help you measure all of the ingredients.

2. Tip the butter and sugar into a large bowl and, using a wooden spoon, mix together until creamy.

3. Carefully break the eggs into the bowl and stir until the eggs are thoroughly mixed in.

4. Using a sieve, sift the flour and baking powder into the bowl. Carefully stir everything together, then spoon the mix into the cupcake cases.

5. Ask an adult to pop the cupcake tray into the oven and bake for 15 minutes, or until golden on top. Then ask an adult to take the tray out and leave the cupcakes to cool on the wire rack.

6. Once the cakes have cooled, use a teaspoon to carefully spoon a little of the centre of the cakes out. Fill the hole in each cake with a teaspoon of jam. Carefully break the small centre of cake into two pieces and place on top of the jam so that it looks like a butterfly.

7. Once you have made all of your cakes, sprinkle some icing sugar over them to make the cupcakes look extra special.

Splishing and Splashing

Deep in the green shade
Two mums sit, lazily chatting.

But Norah and Katie are busy,
Turning the tap,
Filling buckets
And the watering can,
Slooshing in it;
Making mud,
Making rivers and dams
And swimming pools for ants.

Olly's busy too,
Sitting in a basin of water,
Bailing out.

Berry burst ice cubes

These pretty ice cubes are bursting with flavour
and can be added to a drink of water to give it extra zing!

Ingredients:
A little tap water
A handful of blueberries
A handful of raspberries
A bunch of fresh mint

You will need:
An ice cube tray

Method

1. Ask an adult to help you carefully fill the ice cube tray with a little tap water, filling each section about halfway to the top.

2. Place the tray on a flat surface. Wash the berries then drop one berry into each section of the tray.

3. Tear the mint into little pieces and add to the berries.

4. Carefully place the ice cube tray on a flat shelf in the freezer. When the ice cubes have frozen, ask an adult to help you press them out of the tray and add to a drink.

Fruit lollies

Use summer fruits to make these tangy lollies – just make sure that the pieces of fruit are big enough to stay on the stick!

Ingredients:
12 strawberries
1 apple
2 bananas
Makes 6

You will need:
6 wooden lollipop sticks
A knife
A chopping board

Method

1. Remove the stalks from the strawberries. Peel the bananas and carefully chop them into large chunks. Slice the apple into twelve pieces.

2. Carefully slide a piece of fruit onto a lollipop stick, leaving a little room at the bottom of the stick so you can hold on to it.

3. Add more fruit until the stick is full. Repeat for the other sticks.

4. Chill the lollies in the fridge and eat them on the same day.

Sunshine salad

Add some sunshine to mealtimes with this wonderfully fresh and colourful salad. Use as many types of veggies as you'd like!

Ingredients:
100 g shell pasta
Half a cucumber
A red pepper
A small tin of sweetcorn
A bunch of fresh basil
A drizzle of olive oil
Serves 4

You will need:
A chopping board
A knife
A large mixing bowl
A wooden spoon

Method

1. Ask an adult to cook and drain the pasta and leave it to cool. Wash and dry the cucumber and pepper and ask an adult to help you carefully chop the vegetables into small chunks on a chopping board.

2. Ask an adult to drain the sweetcorn and tip it into the bowl with the pasta. Add the cucumber and pepper pieces and use a wooden spoon to mix well together.

3. Use your hands to tear some basil over the pasta. Drizzle a little olive oil over the pasta salad and serve.

Tomato pops

Tomatoes are very juicy and tend to pop a little when you bite into them. They taste yummy with a little bit of basil and cheese.

Ingredients:
6 cherry tomatoes
A bunch of fresh basil
A ball of mozzarella
Makes 12

You will need:
A chopping board
A knife
12 cocktail sticks
A plate for serving

Method

1. Ask an adult to help you chop the tomatoes in half on a chopping board. Tear twelve leaves off the basil. Open the mozzarella packet, drain the excess liquid and tear the mozzarella into twelve little strips.

2. Ask an adult to carefully slide a cherry tomato half onto each cocktail stick, then add a little mozzarella and a basil leaf.

3. Repeat until all of the ingredients are used, then place the tomato pops onto a plate to serve.

Old Bones

At the Natural History Museum,
in the biggest room of all,
there's a huge skeleton.

It is of an animal who lived long ago, as big as a ship
from head to tail, with a great arched neck
and holes where once there were eyes.

And when Olly and Katie are standing
under its tail, looking at its
great teeth, they wonder
what it would be like
to meet an alive one.

But Dad says there
were no people
living in the world then.

Luckily.

Dinosaur crunchies

*These crunchy pastries are perfect sprinkled with
a little cheese on top that turns golden when baked.*

Ingredients:
A little plain flour
A sheet of ready rolled puff pastry
A sprinkle of grated cheese
A little milk
Makes 12

You will need:
A rolling pin
A dinosaur-shaped cutter
A baking tray lined with
  baking paper
A pastry brush
A wire cooling rack

Method

1. Ask an adult to preheat the oven to 180°C and sprinkle
   a little flour onto a clean surface.

2. Roll out the pastry on the floured surface until it is about
   half a centimetre thick.

3. Using your cutter, carefully cut twelve shapes out of the pastry
   and pop them on the tray. If you don't have a dinosaur-shaped
   cutter, don't worry, you can use any shaped cutter you like.

4. Brush each shape with some milk and sprinkle a little cheese
   on top.

5. Ask an adult to pop the tray in the oven for 15 minutes
   or until golden. When the crunchies are baked, ask an adult
   to put them onto a wire rack to cool.

Mega-minty dip

Dunk any kind of veggies into this yummy dip.
It can even be enjoyed with a dinosaur crunchy!

Ingredients:
Half a cucumber
150 g natural yogurt
A teaspoon of lemon juice
A bunch of fresh mint
Carrot sticks

You will need:
A chopping board
A knife
A teaspoon
A small bowl

Method

1. Ask an adult to help you chop the cucumber into little cubes and put in a bowl. Pour in the yogurt and add a teaspoon of lemon juice.

2. Tear up a little mint and sprinkle it into the dip, then mix everything together.

3. Dip your carrot sticks and any leftover cucumber into the dip and enjoy!

Our Cat Ginger

No cat is as nice as Olly
and Katie's cat Ginger.

There's the sleek black
cat with pale green eyes
that they often talk to
on their way to the park,

and there's the big striped
Daddy cat who lives
next door.

There are four little kittens
at their friend Norah's house.

And there's Grandma's beautiful Queenie.

But no cat – *no* cat –
is as nice as Olly
and Katie's
cat Ginger.

Gingerbread paws

Enjoy these crumbly ginger paw biscuits with a glass of milk.

Ingredients:
200 g plain flour
2 teaspoons of ground ginger
A pinch of cinnamon
A teaspoon of baking powder
100 g butter
100 g soft brown sugar
2 tablespoons of golden syrup
Makes 20

You will need:
A large mixing bowl
A wooden spoon
A rolling pin
A small circular cutter
2 baking trays lined with
  baking paper
A wire cooling rack

Method

1. Ask an adult to preheat the oven to 180°C.

2. Add the flour, ginger, cinnamon and baking powder
   into a bowl.

3. Add the butter and rub it into the mix until
   it looks like breadcrumbs.

4. Add the sugar and golden syrup to the bowl
   and mix it all together with your wooden
   spoon to make a soft dough.

5. Cover the dough and leave it to chill in the fridge for 30 minutes.

6. Sprinkle a clean surface that you can reach with some flour. Tip the dough onto the floured surface, then roll it out to about one centimetre thick.

7. Use a cutter to cut circular shapes out of the dough and place them onto the baking trays, making sure to leave room between each biscuit.

8. Use the edge of the cutter to make three lines at the top of each biscuit, so that they look like paws.

9. Ask an adult to put the biscuits into the oven for 12–15 minutes, or until lightly golden-brown, then put the biscuits onto a wire rack to cool.

Saturday Shopping

Saturday is a shopping day.
Olly and Katie don't like shops
much, but they like the market
when the stalls are all lit up,
and there are crowds of people.
Katie holds on tight to Dad's
hand while they load Olly's buggy
with apples, grapes and bananas
and sometimes even a pumpkin.
There are squeaky toys and plastic
balls, T-shirts, watches and sparkling
rings. And they can smell the smell from
the baker's shops, bread, cakes, cookies and
hot pies, tempting them in from the dark street.

Baked apples

*As apples are baked, the skin goes a little wrinkly
and the inside becomes lovely and juicy.*

Ingredients:
2 large cooking apples
A handful of raisins
4 teaspoons of caster sugar
A little butter
2 tablespoons of orange juice
Ice cream to serve
Makes 2

You will need:
A teaspoon
An ovenproof dish
An apple corer

Method

1. Ask an adult to preheat the oven to 180°C. Get an adult to help you core the apples, then place them in the dish.

2. Carefully pop a handful of raisins and a teaspoon of sugar into the middle of each apple then add a little butter to the top.

3. Spoon over the orange juice, then sprinkle each apple with another teaspoon of sugar.

4. Ask an adult to bake the apples in the oven for 30 minutes, or until the skin has gone wrinkly and the juices are bubbling. Once baked leave to cool, then serve with some ice cream.

Oaty cookies

These chewy cookies are packed full of flavour.
Once the cookies have cooled, pile them onto a plate to serve.

Ingredients:
75 g butter
50 g caster sugar
2 tablespoons of golden syrup
A teaspoon of ground cinnamon
A teaspoon of baking powder
100 g porridge oats
100 g plain flour
A handful of raisins
2 tablespoons of milk
Makes 10

You will need:
A wooden spoon
A large mixing bowl
2 baking trays lined
  with baking paper
A tablespoon
A wire cooling rack

Method

1. Ask an adult to preheat the oven to 180°C.

2. Tip the butter, sugar and golden syrup into a mixing bowl
   and mix the ingredients together.

3. Add the cinnamon and baking powder, then tip in the oats, flour
   and raisins. Add the milk and mix together until combined.

4. Use a tablespoon to drop a little mix onto the baking trays and
   repeat, leaving a space between each cookie, until all the mix
   has been used.

5. Ask an adult to put the trays in the oven for 15–20 minutes,
   or until the cookies are golden. Once baked, ask an adult to
   transfer the cookies onto a wire rack to cool.

Fireworks

Hoisted up on shoulders so Katie can see,
They're out late, just Dad and her,
And she's hugging his head in the warm blue dark
As they crane their necks by the lake in the park.
And rockets whoosh through the summer night,
Trailing their tails of glittering light,
Cutting up, up, up across the sky,
Exploding in stars, impossibly high;
And golden fountains pour out showers
Of shimmering rain, like fiery flowers;
Catherine wheels whizz round and round,
Roman candles light the ground,
As Katie stops her ears and gasps and gazes
At a lake on fire and a sky ablaze.

Party pinwheels

*Fill and roll up these pinwheel treats with
any fillings you like – the brighter the better!*

Ingredients:
2 medium-sized tortilla wraps
Your favourite sandwich fillings,
  e.g. cream cheese and ham or
  hummus and fresh basil
Makes 12

You will need:
A chopping board
A teaspoon
A knife

Method

1. Lay a tortilla wrap on a chopping board. Add your sandwich fillings – the softer the better – making sure that they go up to the edges of the tortilla.

2. Starting at one side, lift the wrap a little and carefully roll it as tightly as you can, so that it looks like a long sausage! Repeat steps 1–3 with the other tortilla.

3. Ask an adult to help you cut the sausage shapes into slices, about two centimetres thick. Carefully lie the pinwheels on a plate to serve.

Veggie rockets

*These colourful rockets are bursting with flavour.
Try to pack the vegetables quite closely together to make
the rockets nice and strong.*

Ingredients:
A courgette
A red pepper
A yellow pepper
12 cherry tomatoes
A sprinkle of dried oregano
Makes 6

You will need:
A chopping board
A knife
A large mixing bowl
6 wooden skewers
An ovenproof dish

Method

1. Ask an adult to preheat the oven to 180°C.

2. Ask an adult to help you chop the courgette and peppers into large chunks and place them in a bowl.

3. Carefully push a veggie chunk down the skewer, making sure to leave a little room at the bottom of the stick.

4. Fill the skewers to the top with veggies and lay them in an ovenproof dish. Sprinkle with oregano and ask an adult to cook the rockets in the oven for 30 minutes or until the veggies go a little softer.

5. Leave the rockets to cool, then ask an adult to put them on a plate to serve.

Olly Joins In

Katie is doing ballet! With Amanda and James and Kim and Norah. She's got special pink dancing shoes and white tights and a sticking-out skirt.

When the music plays they stand in a row and bend their knees and point their toes – this way, then this way. They stretch up their arms and dance about.

The mums and dads and grannies sit on chairs and watch. And Olly watches too, sitting on Mum's lap.

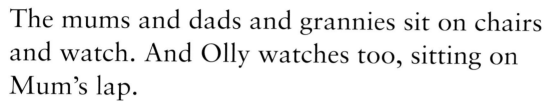

Once, when they were being spring flowers coming out of the ground, Olly joined in and tried to dance too!

Olly doesn't know how to dance properly yet. Katie didn't much like it when he joined in. But nobody else seemed to mind.

Beautiful bow tarts

*Use two halves of a raspberry to make the beautiful bow shapes
for the top of these fruity tarts.*

Ingredients:
A little butter
A little plain flour
A sheet of ready rolled
  shortcrust pastry
Raspberry jam
6 raspberries
A sprinkle of icing sugar
Makes 12

You will need:
A 12-hole cupcake tray
A circular cutter
A teaspoon
A wire cooling rack

Method

1. Ask an adult to preheat the oven to 180°C. Grease the cupcake tray with a little butter.

2. Sprinkle a clean and reachable surface with a little flour. Unroll the pastry onto the surface.

3. Carefully cut twelve circular shapes out of the pastry, wiggling the cutter a little to release each shape from the pastry.

4. Lift the circles into the cupcake tray and push each one down gently so that it touches the bottom and sides. When all of the pastry shapes are in the tray, pop a teaspoon of jam into the centre of each and smooth it down.

5. Ask an adult to bake the bow tarts in the oven for about 15 minutes or until the pastry is golden and the jam starts to bubble. Ask an adult to take the tarts out of the oven and leave to cool on the cooling rack.

6. Wash and dry the raspberries then ask an adult to help you chop them in half. To make the bow shapes, place two raspberry halves on top of each tart, so that the narrower parts of the fruit touch.

7. Sprinkle a little icing sugar over the top of each tart to make them extra special.

Strawberry drops

Strawberries are juicy and delicious just as they are, but you can make them extra special by dipping them in chocolate.

Ingredients:
12 strawberries
100 g milk chocolate
Makes 12

You will need:
A heatproof bowl
A baking tray lined with
   baking paper
A plate for serving

Method

1. Ask an adult to melt the chocolate in a heatproof bowl and leave to cool.

2. Holding each strawberry by its green stalk, carefully lower it into the chocolate until it is covered.

3. Pop the chocolate-covered strawberry onto the tray. Repeat until you have dipped and covered all of the strawberries, then put the tray in the fridge to set.

4. Once the chocolate has set, pop the strawberries onto a plate and serve as a festive treat.

Snowman sweets

Wrap these little sweets in pretty paper and give them to your friends and family at Christmas time.

Ingredients:
150 g white marzipan
8 edible silver balls
Makes 8

You will need:
A chopping board
A knife
A baking tray lined
  with baking paper
A small paintbrush

Method

1. Ask an adult to help you cut the marzipan into two pieces on a chopping board.

2. Cut the two pieces in half so you have four pieces, and then cut those four pieces in half so that you are left with eight.

3. Take one piece of marzipan and break it into two smaller pieces, making sure that one piece is slightly bigger than the other.

4. Roll each piece in your hand to make two balls. Make a smaller ball to go on top of the bigger ball and press down slightly to make a snowman shape.

5. Repeat steps 3–4 to make the rest of your snowmen, then transfer them all to the baking tray.

6. Use the end of a paintbrush to make indents for eyes and a mouth on each snowman sweet, then add a silver ball for the nose.